W9-CFE-279

Weekly Reader Presents

Traveling Matt's Adventures in Outer Space

(Original Title: The Tale of Traveling Matt)

By Michaela Muntean · Pictures by Lisa McCue

Muppet Press
Holt, Rinehart and Winston
NEW YORK

Library of Congress Cataloging in Publication Data
Muntean, Michaela.
The tale of Traveling Matt.
Summary: A fraggle ponders on the adventures of his
uncle Matt in the outside world as he meets for the first
time cows, garbage trucks, and people.
[1. Stories in rhyme]   I. McCue, Lisa, ill.   II. Title.
PZ8.3.M89Tal 1984   [E]   83-23711
ISBN 0-03-071092-8
First Edition
Printed in the United States of America
1 3 5 7 9 10 8 6 4 2

ISBN 0-03-071092-8

This book is a presentation of
Weekly Reader Books

Weekly Reader Books offers book clubs for children
from preschool through junior high school.

For further information write to:
Weekly Reader Books
4343 Equity Drive
Columbus, Ohio 43228

THROUGH a dark and twisting tunnel,
Past a dank and dripping cave,
Treads a Fraggle who is known to be
The bravest of the brave....

Past Fraggle Pond where Fraggles play—
Past boulder, stream, and stone—
Past all we love in Fraggle Rock
Into the Great Unknown—

Goes that fearless, hardy Fraggle
With his backpack and his hat,
Goes that traveler of all travelers—
It's my Uncle Traveling Matt!

When I asked why he wanted
To leave for who-knows-where,
Matt scratched his head and then he said,
"Why, just because it's there!

"The ancient lore of Fraggle Rock
Describes another place—
A place that's far beyond the Rock.
I call it Outer Space.

"I plan to study Outer Space
I'll listen and I'll look.
I'll keep good notes and records
(And maybe write a book)."

I am Matt's only nephew
(Gobo Fraggle is my name),
And someday, maybe someday
I will try to do the same.

But now it's Uncle Traveling Matt
Who turns and says good-bye,
And me—that's Gobo—left behind
To heave a farewell sigh.

"Young Gobo, I will not forget
The Fraggles left behind.
I'll send you many postcards that
Describe the things I find!"

And with that promise, Matt sets out
To face what he must face—
All the danger and excitement
In the world of Outer Space!

"Dear Gobo, I've examined
All the things that I can see.
The creatures here are very strange....
They're not like you and me.

"I wrote this postcard from a place
With grass and sky and ground.
A number of inhabitants
Were wandering around.

"I noticed one large group of folks
Who had a thoughtful look,
So from my pack I quickly pulled
My pencil and my book.

"I was ready with my questions.
I began my interview.
But the only thing they answered
Was a slow and steady *moo*.

" 'Who?' I said, and 'Moo-moo, too!'
But that's as far as it went.
The next group only answered *quack*
And who knows what *that* meant!

"Dear Gobo, I was sure I'd met
The strangest creatures here.
But then I saw one stranger yet—
Who filled me full of fear.

"A giant beast on giant wheels
With terrifying might.
A mouth of teeth that opened wide
Consuming all in sight!

"Dear Gobo, there are creatures here
Who talk and sing all day!
(Although they never listen to
A single word I say.)

"They seem to be quite pleasant
But they're lazy as can be
They never seem to move an inch—
At least that I can see!

"Dear Gobo, there are beings here
Who really are bizarre.
I call them Silly Creatures.
(That's exactly what they are!)

They seem to live on land or sea,
And even in the air!
"I've seen them wear disguises
I've seen them everywhere.

"Some are tall, and some are small
And some are thin or fat.
I'll keep collecting data.
Love, your Uncle Traveling Matt."

So somewhere, somewhere, way out there
In the World Beyond,
Far away from Fraggle Rock
And far from Fraggle Pond

Treads a lone and fearless Fraggle.
The Fraggle who is that
Brave and true adventurer
My Uncle Traveling Matt!